Where Does a Tiger-Heron Spend the Night?

Written by Margaret Carney

Illustrated by Mélanie Watt

Kids Can Press

Where does a tiger-heron spend the night?

Where does a storm-petrel live out its days?

Deep in the mangroves,
tucked out of sight.

What does a toucan most like to eat?

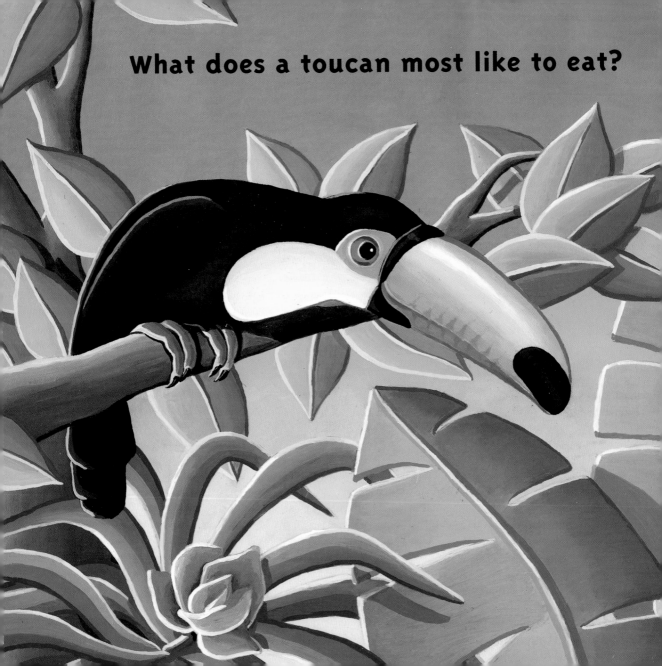

Skimming the crests
of the ocean waves.

Why does an osprey plunge from the sky?

Wild figs
and mangoes,
juicy and sweet.

To grasp a fat catfish
it spies swimming by.

How does a lyrebird learn how to sing?

By mimicking other birds
warbling in spring.

Why does a hummingbird hover mid-air?

How does a nightjar keep safe during day?

To sip from
the trumpetvine
dangling there.

It lies like a lump
on a limb in the shade.

Why does a spoonbill have such a broad beak?

To slurp up small shrimp
with each side-to-side sweep.

What snacks does a roadrunner grind in its gizzard?

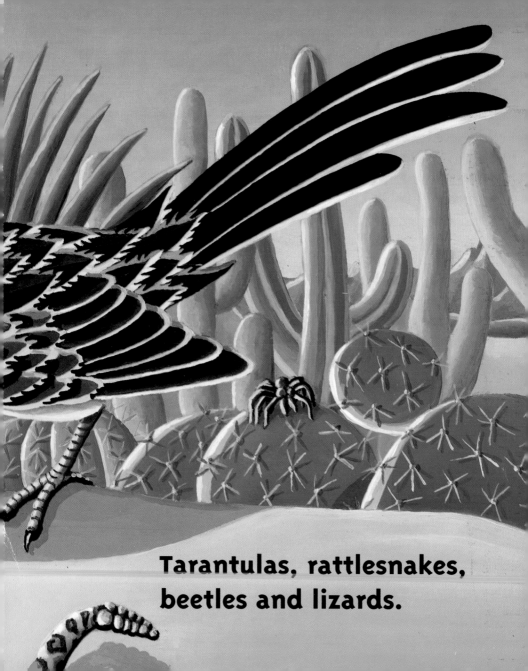

Tarantulas, rattlesnakes,
beetles and lizards.

How does a ptarmigan hide from its foe?

Its brown summer feathers
turn white with the snow.

Why does a vulture soar high overhead?

It's sniffing the wind
for the scent of the dead.

Where does a whimbrel
leave prints in the sand?

**All round the planet,
on each ocean strand.**

Tiger-heron

The handsome striped feathers of a tiger-heron look like a tiger's fur — that's how it got its name. Tiger-herons live alone, hiding among mangrove trees at the edge of the sea. By feeding mostly at night, they escape predators like hawks and eagles, but they still have to watch out for jaguars! When tiger-herons sense danger, they point their bills toward the sky, making them look like the pointed roots of a mangrove.

Storm-petrel

The smallest of seabirds, storm-petrels flutter close to the surface of the ocean, feeding on plankton and krill. Their special tubenose bills allow them to drink seawater and get rid of the salt. Like albatrosses, storm-petrels travel for months at sea and sleep on the water. Sometimes they take shelter behind ships in a storm, which is how they got their name.

Toucan

The toucan lives in rain forest treetops. Too heavy to perch on thin twigs, it lands on a thicker limb and reaches out with its long beak to pluck fruit growing at the tip. With a toss of its head, the toucan throws the fruit into its throat and swallows it. Toucans with the biggest, most colorful bills have the best success finding mates.

Osprey

With their large, round eyes, ospreys see three times better than humans. Soaring high above water, these "fish hawks" fold their wings and dive with a splash when they spot a fish, grabbing it with their spiny clawed toes. Ospreys tear a big fish into little pieces with their sharp hooked beaks before feeding it to their babies.

Lyrebird

Lyrebirds have an amazing ability to copy sounds made by other birds in the Australian rain forest. They even imitate barking dogs and honking cars. A male lyrebird attracts a mate with his loud, ringing song, then shows off by raising his long, feathered tail and shaking it. When raised, the tail plumes look like a lyre — a U-shaped harp.

Hummingbird

A hummingbird pokes its long, thin bill deep into a flower, sticks out its even longer tongue and soaks up nectar with the brushy tip. Hummingbirds drink lots of nectar — half their weight each day — to keep their tiny bodies warm and to refuel for flying. They not only hover in front of flowers, they're the only birds able to fly backward! Their wings beat 80 times each second — so fast you can't see them move. The hum of their vibrating feathers gives hummingbirds their name.

Nightjar

Whip-poor-wills, nighthawks and other nightjars fly through the dark sky, hunting their favorite food: moths. Their beaks are short, but their jaws have special hinges that allow them to open amazingly wide. Nightjars also sing at night to attract mates. Instead of building a nest, they lay their eggs on the ground. Mottled gray feathers provide nightjars with perfect camouflage by day, as they sit on their eggs or doze on a tree limb.

Spoonbill

A spoonbill relies on its sense of touch to find food, especially in muddy water or at night. It sweeps its spoon-shaped bill back and forth through the water of a shallow marsh, and when it feels a shrimp, small fish or water beetle against the sensitive tip, it snaps it up. Most spoonbills have white feathers, but roseate spoonbills have beautiful pink feathers because of pigments in the food they eat.

Roadrunner

Because everything it eats moves fast, a roadrunner must run even faster to catch its dinner. Having big feet, long legs and short stubby wings, it runs much better than it flies. A roadrunner is quick enough to kill a rattlesnake without being bitten, and often runs about with part of a snake hanging out of its mouth, digesting it bit by bit. Roadrunners often nest in a thorny shrub or cactus for protection from hawks.

Ptarmigan

Ptarmigan (pronounced *tar-ma-gun*) live in the Arctic and on mountaintops, where there are no trees to hide in. But as the seasons change, so does the color of their feathers, matching the land around them. When a hungry fox lopes by, a ptarmigan stays as still as a stone — and looks like one. Feathers on their feet keep their toes warm in winter and act like snowshoes.

Vulture

Turkey vultures have just about the keenest sense of smell of any bird, and they use it to find food far away. Other vultures, even king vultures and condors, have learned to follow them. All vultures have bald heads, allowing them to eat dead animals without dirtying their feathers. They also have strong digestive systems that kill germs, so they don't get sick from eating rotten meat.

Whimbrel

At different times of the year, whimbrels can be found on beaches of every continent in the world except Antarctica. They breed in the far north, then migrate as far south as Chile and Tasmania. Among the largest of shorebirds, whimbrels use their long, curved beaks to probe in mud for worms and in water for small shrimp and fish. Whimbrels are known for their lovely, haunting calls.

For Mary Lauer Thometz Carney, my mom,
who loved birds, poetry and reading bedtime stories to children — M.C.

To my grandmothers,
Marie-Anne Leblanc and Edna Watt — M.W.

Text © 2002 Margaret Carney
Illustrations © 2002 Mélanie Watt

Kids Can Press acknowledges the financial support of the Ontario Arts Council, the Canada Council for the Arts and the Government of Canada, through the BPIDP, for our publishing activity.

Published in Canada by
Kids Can Press Ltd.
29 Birch Avenue
Toronto, ON M4V 1E2

Published in the U.S. by
Kids Can Press Ltd.
2250 Military Road
Tonawanda, NY 14150

www.kidscanpress.com

The artwork in this book was rendered in acrylic.
The text is set in Tempus Sans and Triplex.

Edited by Tara Walker
Designed by Mélanie Watt and Marie Bartholomew
Printed in Hong Kong by Wing King Tong Company Limited

This book is singer sewn casebound.
CM 02 0 9 8 7 6 5 4 3 2 1

NATIONAL LIBRARY OF CANADA CATALOGUING IN PUBLICATION DATA

Carney, Margaret (Margaret Rose), (date).
Where does a tiger-heron spend the night?

ISBN 1-55337-022-8

1. Birds — Miscellanea — Juvenile literature. I. Watt, Mélanie, 1975— II. Title.

QL676.2.C37 2002   j598   C2001-901748-0

Kids Can Press is a Nelvana company